The Children's Menu

GRETA GORSUCH

Greta Gorsuch taught ESL/EFL and Applied Linguistics for forty years in Japan, Vietnam, and the US. Her research has appeared in academic journals. She is currently coeditor of *Reading in a Foreign Language*. Her books in the Gemma Open Door series include *Newcomers, Post Office on the Tokaido, The Cell Phone Lot,* and *The Night Telephone.* Greta lives in Iowa, where she continues her work for new readers.

First published by Gemma in 2025.

www.gemmamedia.org

Printed in the United States of America

978-1-956476-39-2

Library of Congress Cataloging-in-Publication Data

Names: Gorsuch, Greta, author.
Title: The children's menu / Greta Gorsuch.
Boston : Gemma, 2025. | Series: Gemma open door |
Identifiers: LCCN 2024054792 (print) | LCCN 2024054793 (ebook) | ISBN
9781956476392 (paperback) | ISBN 9781956476408 (epub)
Subjects: LCGFT: High interest-low vocabulary books. | Novels.
Classification: LCC PS3607.O77 C48 2025 (print) | LCC PS3607.
O77 (ebook) |
DDC 813/.6--dc23/eng/20241204
LC record available at https://lccn.loc.gov/2024054792
LC ebook record available at https://lccn.loc.gov/2024054793

Cover by Laura Shaw Design

Named after the brightest star in the Northern Crown, Gemma is a nonprofit organization that helps new readers acquire English language literacy skills with relevant, engaging books, eBooks, and audiobooks. Always original, never adapted, these stories introduce adults and young adults to the life-changing power of reading.

Open Door

Henry was a medium-sized boy. He was like any of the kids at Circletown Elementary School. His class filled the big room in the big building. Thirty of them, boys and girls, all nine and ten years old.

His friend Jake was the first to say something. "Henry," he said, "What's going on at your house?" He turned around in his desk to talk to Henry. Mrs. Hambrake was talking to another teacher at the classroom door and did not see.

Henry did have an answer for Jake. But he did not want to talk. Maybe Jake would forget his question.

But Jake was not forgetting. Jake said, "All those boxes and things? That moving truck? Are you leaving?"

"I'm not leaving," said Henry.

"Oh, OK," said Jake.

Henry looked down at his book. He was reading a story, sort of. He could not keep his eyes on it. Usually, Henry loved to read. Just not today.

School was a good place for Henry. He knew what happened at school. You had classes. You had math. You had reading. You had geography. Henry and his classmates laughed at the maps in geography class. Everyone knew that maps did not work in Circletown. In fact, Mrs. Hambrake had been thirty minutes late to school every day this week. She kept getting lost. The roads in

Circletown went anywhere they liked. They seemed to change overnight. This morning, the police had to find Mrs. Hambrake. She arrived at school in the back of a police car. She was laughing, but she also looked sick.

Sports at school were good, too. But lunch at school was not so good. Henry would not eat much. He might eat a little meat. He would drink the milk. Henry was a very picky eater. No fruit. No vegetables. Nothing that looked or smelled strange. No one at school said anything about what Henry ate or what he did not eat.

Henry knew what happened at school. It was safe.

Until two weeks ago, home was a good place for Henry. Now he did not feel that way. Henry closed his eyes. There was no point in reading the story in front of him. He did not care what Mrs. Hambrake might say.

Chapter Two

Henry told Jake the truth. Henry was not leaving his house. Henry's dad was gone, though. He had left the house two weeks ago. Half of the things in the house were gone. The sofa and the TV were gone. Henry's mother, Dr. Berniece Baker, did not say anything about the missing things. She did not say anything about Henry's dad. But both Henry and his mother had started eating in the kitchen. Their big dining room table was gone. Henry's dad had taken it.

Before his dad left, home was a lot like school for Henry. He knew how the days would go. On school days, he woke up and smelled his mother's coffee. He went downstairs and found some milk to drink. He found some white bread to eat. At the dining room table, Dr. Berniece Baker read the newspaper and would say, "Good morning, Henry." She would not look up. His dad would come in. He would see Henry drinking milk and eating white bread. He would then put more things on the table to eat. "Here. Try this," his dad would say. It might be strawberry jam or a banana. Sometimes Henry would take a little cheese. Then he would hide it under his plate. Henry's dad saw this. He would smile.

After a few minutes of chewing on toast or eggs, Henry's dad might say, "Henry, I think I hear someone at the door. Go look."

Henry would go look. There would be no one there, of course. Henry would come back to the dining room. "No one there," he would say.

Henry would sit down and pick up his piece of white bread and eat some. On the bottom of the white bread would be some jam or peanut butter. While Henry was at the door, his dad would put it on Henry's bread. It was his trick to get Henry to eat more than white bread. Henry and his dad would laugh. Henry did not like jam or peanut butter, but he would eat the bread anyway. It made his dad happy. Henry loved it.

Now, Henry's dad was gone. Breakfasts felt half empty, like the house. No more tricks with the front door and peanut butter on white bread. There was just Henry and his mother and her newspaper. Worse, a few times his mother had put her newspaper down. She looked at what Henry was eating. It was as if she was seeing Henry's milk and white bread for the first time. This feeling made Henry want to leave the table.

Then came the morning when Henry's mom put down her newspaper and looked at him.

"Henry," said his mom. "Summer break is beginning next month. I have to teach. I'm also writing my play. I won't be around very much. Someone needs to stay with you. I have found someone."

It took Henry a minute to understand. Then he did understand. A *babysitter*, thought Henry.

Chapter Three

Corey arrived the next morning. Henry was at the kitchen table. Today, his white bread and milk did not taste right.

Henry had not slept. He had too many thoughts in his head. One: His dad was gone. Two: School was ending next month. Summer break was not going to be as he thought. Three: His mom got him a *babysitter*. What would his friends say?

Every few minutes, Henry saw his mother's hand reach out from behind the newspaper. She picked up her coffee. Henry heard her drink her coffee. Then, for the first time, Henry heard something new. Dr. Berniece Baker made a happy sound. It was a little *ahhhh* sound. Did his mom like coffee that much? She drank one or two cups every morning. Henry took a drink from his glass of milk. It tasted OK now. But it was nothing to make a happy sound about. What would happen if he put a little coffee into his milk?

He was about to ask his mother about that. But then, Henry's mother said, "I think I heard someone at the door."

"What?" Henry asked. Was this a joke? This was the kind of trick his dad played. Dr. Berniece Baker did not make jokes. She did not play tricks.

Then Henry heard a knock on the door. He got up from the table. He walked through the half empty living room. He stopped at the front door.

"Is everything OK?" Dr. Berniece Baker called from the kitchen. "Open the door."

Henry opened the door.

Henry looked at the tallest girl he had ever seen. If Henry stood as tall as he could, he reached the girl's middle. The girl looked down at Henry. She was not smiling, but she looked like she could. This girl *felt* quiet. She did not move as she looked at Henry. There was no need to talk. Henry liked it. The morning had become interesting.

Henry heard his mother walk up behind.

"Hi, Corey," said Dr. Berniece Baker.

"Hi, Dr. Baker," said the girl, now named Corey. "I thought I'd walk Henry to school. It's on the way for me."

Henry's mom said, "Good idea." She said to Henry, "This is Corey Turnbridge. She'll be looking after you this summer."

Before Henry knew what was happening, his mother handed him his school backpack. She pushed him out the door and said, "Have a good day!"

Corey (the *babysitter*??) used her arm to make a slow, wide, sweeping gesture that said, *"Come on, let's go."*

Chapter Four

Henry was walking to school with a *girl*. Yes, she was maybe sixteen or seventeen, but she was *still a girl*. She walked and said nothing.

They walked under tall trees that were green with new leaves. School would be out next month, but spring came late to Circletown, Indiana.

Corey had come early to Henry's house. There was still lots of time before the school bell rang. They were walking slowly. Corey seemed to be in no hurry. She looked around as she walked.

Circletown was old. There were giant houses next to tiny houses, and narrow twisting streets. Streets ended in odd places like a park or a quiet cemetery. There were lots of surprises in Circletown.

Henry said to Corey, "You smell like a swimming pool."

Corey laughed. Then, she said, "I had swim practice. My hair is still wet from the pool."

Henry said, "Swim practice?"

Corey nodded. "Every morning at five."

Henry said slowly, "You're a swimmer. At school. On the team."

Corey said, "Uh-huh. The 400 meter and 800 meter races."

Henry just looked at her. *Wow*, he thought. *A girl who does sports.*

"In the summer," Corey said, "I go wild swimming."

Henry wondered what "wild swimming" was. He was about to ask when Corey said, "I'm hungry. I haven't had breakfast. Let's get something to eat." Without waiting for Henry to answer, she turned down a street to the right. Henry was not sure, but he thought they were headed to Mound Street. It was the busiest street in Circletown. He followed Corey. It was still early. School could wait.

They did not walk far. They took a right turn down a little street, then went down a hill and around a corner, and there was Mound Street. Circletown was like that. The streets went anywhere they liked. You never knew where you might end up. Usually,

Henry kept to the few streets he knew well. He liked to feel safe. But today, he felt different.

The shop Corey wanted to go to was called Jet Coffee. Henry had lived in Circletown most of his life. He did not remember seeing this shop before.

Corey opened the door. They went inside.

Chapter Five

Jet Coffee was quiet. The floor and walls were wood. A few people were sitting at wood tables. All of the wood had its own color, some of it light brown and some of it dark.

Henry could see lots of cars and people on Mound Street outside. People were on their way to work and to school. Still, Jet Coffee was quiet inside. Henry smelled wood and coffee. For a few seconds, he could not move. It was like having a strong memory but not knowing what the memory was.

Corey walked to the back of the café. Henry followed. There was a long table there. A man with black hair stood behind it. Behind him were wood shelves with coffee cups and plates. It was a kitchen. There was a large wood tub with a white towel on top. At the other end of the table, Henry saw a shiny machine. There was steam coming out of it.

Corey was talking to the man. Corey then said, "Henry, this is my boss, Hiroto Maru."

Henry said, "Your boss?" Henry was talking a lot this morning. He was not used to it.

Corey said, "Yes. I work here after school."

The man's eyes were dark. The man was small, but looked very strong.

Corey said, "He is Maru-sensei. He's teaching me to cook and to make coffee." She looked at the man and said, "Maru-sensei, this is Henry."

Henry said, "Hello, Maru-sensei."

The man said, "Hello, Henry." The man did not smile. Yet there was something friendly about him.

Corey said quietly, "Can you bow a little? Like this." She bent her back and neck. Her head nodded forward. Henry copied her. The man nodded back.

Corey said, "Maru-sensei, may I make some *onigiri* and coffee *gyunyu* for Henry and me to take to school? I had swim practice this morning."

Maru-sensei said, "Go ahead. You can show Henry how. The rice is fresh." He pointed to the wood tub. "There are some plums in the refrigerator. They arc ready to eat."

Henry asked Corey, "What are you doing?"

Corey led Henry behind the long table. "We're making rice balls for breakfast."

Henry felt unsafe. This was too much. Meeting his babysitter? A girl who did sports? Eating rice? And plums? The morning was falling apart.

Corey said, "It's OK, Henry. We still have time before school. We'll eat on the way." She showed him how to wash his hands at the metal sink. Then she said, "Breakfast time."

Chapter Six

Corey and Henry made the rice balls first. Corey took warm piles of white rice out of the tub. She put the steaming rice on a wood board. Then, she took a bowl out of the refrigerator. Finally, she took down a box from a shelf. She opened it and took out a sheet of dark green paper. She held the paper for Henry to touch.

Henry asked, "What's that?"

Corey answered, "That's *nori*. Seaweed. We put it around the *onigiri*. It holds the rice together. It also gives it a good taste."

Henry stepped back.

Corey said, "I'll tell you what. Think of this. Do you like salt?"

Henry said, "I guess."

Corey said, "This seaweed is salty. You can touch it again. Then put your finger on your tongue and taste."

Henry touched the seaweed. He put his finger to his tongue. He tasted salt. And he tasted something else. It was not bad.

Maru-sensei was back. Both he and Corey wet their hands with water.

Corey said, "The rice won't stick to your hands if they are wet."

Maru-sensei and Corey each held some rice in their hands. They turned the rice into a kind of ball. Corey picked out a small red fruit from the bowl. She pushed the fruit into the center of the rice ball.

She said, "It's a plum. It's salty and sour."

Maru-sensei took the rice ball Corey had been making. Then he took a piece of the *nori* and wrapped it around the rice ball.

Maru-sensei said to Henry, "This is *onigiri* with plum." To Corey, he said, "I'll show Henry how to make coffee *gyunyu*. Can you make two more *onigiri*?"

Maru-sensei took Henry to the machine. Maru-sensei took out a shining silver cup. Into it, he poured milk. He put the silver cup up to the machine. The machine made noise. Steam rose into the air. Maru-sensei watched the milk in the cup carefully.

After a minute, Maru-sensei turned off the machine. He showed Henry the cup. The milk inside was steaming. It had bubbles on top. Maru-sensei then carefully poured the milk into two paper cups. He took a glass with very dark brown coffee at the bottom and put a spoon of the coffee into each paper cup. He stirred the coffee into the hot milk. He added a little sugar into Henry's cup.

Maru-sensei said, "Coffee *gyunyu*. 'Coffee milk,' as they say in my country." He handed Henry his paper cup.

Chapter Seven

Mound Street was busy with cars. Kids were walking to school. Yellow school buses went by.

After the quiet café, it was noisy. Henry did not care. He was having his first cup of coffee milk. It was like closing his eyes. He could stop the world. Only now, his eyes were open. He was smelling and tasting. He felt warm inside. It was not like drinking cold milk. It was not like eating a piece of white bread.

Henry jumped a little when Corey asked, "Do you like your coffee *gyunyu?*" She was drinking her coffee milk with one hand and eating her rice ball with the other. They were walking slowly on Mound Street to school. Henry's school was just a few minutes away. Corey's high school was behind Henry's school, up a hill.

Henry said, "Yes!"

Corey laughed. "Yes?"

Henry said, "I mean, I like it."

Corey said, "Good." She finished her rice ball. She was hungry after swim practice. There was no food at home. Her dad was gone a lot. Corey's mom was years gone. And her brother Mark? He was no brother at all.

Corey started on her second rice ball. After a few minutes of walking and eating, she said, "I have to work after school. I'll see you tomorrow morning again. We can go to school together.

Maru-sensei likes you. If you want, we can try to make some breakfast soup."

Henry said loudly, "Soup?" He had to shout a little because another school bus was going by. Henry's friend Jake was on it. Jake was watching Henry. Henry was walking with a tall teenage girl to school!

Corey said, "Yes. Maru-sensei is from Japan. He says they eat different things for breakfast than we do. In Japan, they eat soup for breakfast. Are you going to eat your rice ball?"

Henry was not sure he wanted to. Coffee *gyunyu* was enough new stuff for one day. He handed his rice ball to Corey.

Corey said, "I'll pull off one piece for you. You should try a little."

She took the rest of Henry's rice ball. She turned and started to walk to the high school up the hill. She was eating the rice ball as she walked. Henry thought, *She's really hungry. It must be from swim practice.*

He looked at the piece of rice ball in his hand. Very slowly, he put it in his mouth. It was sweet, salty, and soft.

The school bell rang. Henry needed to get inside.

In Henry's class, the kids made a lot of noise. Henry's friends were talking about him.

Henry was not surprised when Jake asked, "Who was that girl you were walking with?"

Henry said, "It's Corey." He would not say more.

Chapter Eight

Summer vacation would start tomorrow. The kids in school could not wait for vacation to begin. Everyone wanted to be outside. Four or five teachers got lost on their way to school. Two *school buses* got lost.

"I turned down my usual street and suddenly I was in the middle of a cornfield," said one bus driver to the police. "I don't know how *that* happened!"

Henry's classmates could not stay in their desks. Mrs. Hambrake was starting to look bad. Some girls in Henry's class chased a cat up a tree. They laughed and shouted until Mrs. Hambrake came to see. Mrs. Hambrake sent the girls away. She talked to the cat. Mrs.

Hambrake got the cat down, but then she also got dirt on her dress.

Jake shook his head. "Girls are trouble," he said.

Henry thought about that. He thought girls *were* trouble. But *boys* were trouble, too. Jake broke a window at home with a baseball. Jake's dad was making him work at his television shop downtown to pay for it.

These past weeks, Henry was drinking coffee milk and eating rice balls and breakfast soup with Corey. He was trying new foods. Somehow, being at Jet Coffee made it OK to try new things.

One day, Maru-sensei laid out tuna and mayonnaise for the rice balls.

Henry said, "Mayonnaise?" That was something Henry's mom put on her chicken sandwiches or her hamburgers. But on tuna?

Corey said, "Try some tuna without mayonnaise on a little rice."

Henry did. It was OK.

Then Corey said, "Now try some tuna *with* mayonnaise and a little rice."

Henry tried that. It was good with the warm rice. That was the first day Henry ate one whole *onigiri* before school.

*****

Today at school, Mrs. Hambrake let everyone out for lunch. Jake and Henry and their friends played catch with a few baseballs they had. One girl, Allison, wanted to play. Jake said no, but Henry said, "Come on, let her try."

Girls could play catch. He and Corey had played catch a few times in Henry's backyard.

Allison did OK. Then Allison said, "There's that cat again." She pointed.

Henry saw it. It was the little black and white cat some of the girls had chased up a tree. It sat at the edge of the school yard, alone.

After school, Henry found the little cat. Henry still had part of a tuna and mayonnaise rice ball. He gave it to the cat. It stayed at his feet and looked up with big eyes. He picked it up and carried it home. Dr. Berniece Baker was going to have a surprise.

Chapter Nine

Dr. Berniece Baker *was* surprised. But not at first. It took her two days to notice the little black and white cat. After checking in a book, Henry learned that the cat was a girl cat.

Henry had been feeding her in the kitchen. He found two dishes for her. One was for water. Another was for food. The cat had been sleeping on Henry's bed. What was her name? Henry did not know.

Corey was busy with exams at high school. Henry had not seen her. He could not ask her for ideas on names for the little girl cat.

Henry's mom had been away a lot. She left early in the morning and came home late. But this morning when Henry got up, Dr. Berniece Baker was at the kitchen table. She set down her newspaper and said, "Good morning, Henry."

Henry said, "Um …. morning." He was not completely awake. Was the cat on his bed when he got up? He was not sure. He would check later. Right now, he was hungry.

Henry wanted coffee *gyunyu*. He was not at Jet Coffee. He did not have the steaming machine at the back of the café to use. But he thought he could make coffee milk at home. Would his mom give him a little of her coffee to add to his milk?

Henry got out some milk from the refrigerator. Then he got out a small pan. He put some milk into the pan and put it on the stove to warm. He got out a cup. Then he waited. Maru-sensei told Henry you should never hurry when warming milk.

Dr. Berniece Baker watched all of this. Her newspaper lay on the table.

After a few minutes, Henry turned to his mother and asked, "Do you think I could have a little coffee to put in my cup?" His mother smiled at him. He said, "What?"

Dr. Berniece Baker did not answer. She stood up. She started making a fresh cup of coffee. She then said, "Yes, of course. You can have some of this fresh coffee so your coffee will be hot. Will a half cup be enough?"

Henry said, "I think so."

Henry's mom said, "All right, then."

They stood in the kitchen, side by side. They waited for Henry's milk to warm up. They waited for the coffee maker to make a fresh, strong, hot cup of coffee.

Then Dr. Berniece Baker gave a small yelp. "What *is* that?" she said. She looked down. The small black and white cat was rubbing against her legs.

Henry said, "Um …. I found her at school." He closed his eyes.

Henry's mom did not say anything for a few minutes. Then she said, "We should give her a bath. She isn't very clean. Does she have a name?"

Henry opened his eyes. Then he said, "Not yet."

Henry's mom picked up the cat. The cat purred. Dr. Berniece Baker said, "She does have a white spot here that looks like a bell. What about the name 'Bell?'"

Henry said, "OK. Bell."

Henry and his mother had forgotten the newspaper on the table. The open page had a story: "Man Accused of Stealing Cars. Mark Turnbridge, 23, is in jail for stealing cars and trucks in Circletown."

Chapter Ten

After breakfast, Henry decided to walk around Circletown. Henry's mom washed half the breakfast dishes. Henry washed the other half of the dishes. Bell the cat watched from on top of the refrigerator.

Dr. Berniece Baker said, "I'm off to work. I'll see you tonight. Call if you need anything."

It was a bright sunny day. Henry wanted to be outside. But where should he go? He could just start walking. The streets of Circletown were so strange. You did not know where you would end up. Any street looked straight at first. You thought it would take you to a certain place. But then it did not.

It took you to a completely different place. Perhaps it took you up a hill to an old house. Perhaps the street ended against a huge rock, and then around the rock into a forest. Perhaps the street took you to the beautiful Circletown library. The next time you took the same street, and it took you to the high bridge near city hall. The people of Circletown were often late to school or to work. Everyone knew that Circletown streets did not take you where you thought they should go.

Today, Henry thought that was just fine.

He left the house and started walking. He walked under the old, tall trees. They seemed so green. He felt both sunshine and shade as he walked under them. He walked past houses big and small. He saw kids playing in their front yards. He walked by Jake's big white house. He thought to stop in. Then he remembered Jake was working at his dad's television shop downtown. If Circletown's streets took Henry downtown today, he would go see Jake.

Henry turned left down a street he had not seen before. It had a sign at the corner that said "Turnbridge Street." *Turnbridge?* Henry thought. *That's Corey's name.* The street went down a steep hill. There were only a few small houses on the street.

As Henry got to the bottom of the hill, he came to one house that had many cars and trucks around it. They were parked in the yard and on the street. Some were missing windows. Some had grass growing high around them. Henry thought some of those cars would not drive anywhere. He wondered who lived in the house with its forest of junk cars.

Henry saw that downtown was close. He could see city hall and the county courthouse with its big clock. Jake's dad's shop would be on the courthouse square. He walked a little more and found Mound Street. He then crossed the high bridge over the river into downtown.

The county courthouse sat large in the center of Courthouse Square. It was the center of Circletown. Today the courthouse was busy. A lot of people stood around it. Some men were being led out of the courthouse by police officers. The men were walking slowly. They had chains on their feet. The men were prisoners from the jail. The officers were taking the prisoners to cars and putting them inside. Henry was curious and moved closer.

One of the prisoners was tall and young with light hair. He saw Henry looking. He laughed and said, "What're you lookin' at? This ain't the children's menu."

One of the police officers said to the prisoner, "Shut up, Turnbridge. Get in the car."

The young prisoner laughed again. Henry shivered. He felt cold. Then he felt a hand on his shoulder. He jumped, and nearly yelled out in surprise.

It was Jake. He said, "Henry, what are you doing here?"

Chapter Eleven

"Hey Jake," Henry said. Henry's heart was beating fast. The tall prisoner with the light hair had scared him. Then Jake had surprised him by coming out of nowhere.

Jake asked again, "What are you doing here?" He looked at the prisoners and the police officers. "This isn't a good place."

Jake always said what he thought. Sometimes, though, Henry wished Jake said what he thought less loudly. Henry heard more laughter. The tall prisoner had heard Jake! That laughter had a cold sound! It was the sound of someone who wanted to hurt you. Henry said to Jake, "Let's get out of here."

The two boys turned and walked to a shop that said: "Harlow's Courthouse Square Television Shop."

As usual, Jake had questions for Henry. "Why were you watching those guys? They're going to jail, you know."

Henry said, "Oh."

Jake was still talking. "You need to say away from that Mark Turnbridge. He was the one laughing at you. He's no good. He'll hurt you if he can. He doesn't know your name, does he? You didn't talk to him, did you?"

Henry was surprised. He asked Jake, "No. Did you say Turnbridge?"

Jake said, "Yeah, Turnbridge. Turn-bridges are an old family in Circletown. You have to be careful around them. Maybe they were important once. First family in Circletown, and all. Now they steal stuff. Cars, trucks, who knows what else? They're bad news."

"Oh," Henry said.

They had gotten to Jake's dad's television store. The big windows were full of televisions of all sizes. All of them were on.

"Be careful," Jake said. "Hambrake's in there. That's why I got out of there. It's enough I had her at school, but during summer break too? Anyway, I had a feeling you were around."

Sure enough, Mrs. Hambrake was in the shop looking for a new television. Henry said "hello" to her, and she said "hello" back. With a dress, hat, and handbag, she looked like any other shopper.

Jake's dad, Mr. Harlow, said "hi" to Henry. He asked "How's everything at home, Henry? Anything I can do to help?"

Henry thought, *Help? Help with what?* But he said, "Oh, we're OK, Mr. Harlow. Corey is going to come every day."

Mr. Harlow looked at Henry for a minute. He asked, "Corey? You mean Corey Turnbridge, the swimmer?"

"Yes, sir. We're learning to cook. We go to Jet Coffee. She works there," Henry said.

Jake was surprised. "*You*, Henry Baker? Learn to *cook*?"

Mr. Harlow said, "Jet Coffee is a good place. Just be careful how you get there. The streets in Circletown lately…well…they change a lot. You think they'll take you one place. But then they take you someplace else."

Mrs. Hambrake's voice came from the front of the store. She said, "I heard that! It's true. Circletown's streets are strange right now. It took me twenty minutes to get here this morning. I don't know what's happening with these streets of ours!"

Chapter Twelve

Corey came the next day. High school was out for the summer. High school swim practice was over, too. Dr. Berniece Baker had already left for work.

Corey looked the same. Henry also thought she looked tired. Perhaps it was high school exams. Henry thought too of yesterday at the county court-house. That laughing young man was named Turnbridge, just like Corey. And he looked like Corey. But he was rough. He scared Henry. Corey did not scare Henry.

Today, Henry could see gray clouds in the sky when he opened the front door to let Corey in. It might rain.

Corey told Henry, "In a few weeks, it'll be warm enough to go wild swimming. You can try it. Can you swim?" Henry could swim. He learned in the city pool. But he did not know what "wild swimming" was. He asked Corey about it.

Corey said, "Oh, it's swimming in natural places. Like in rivers or creeks or lakes. It's fun!"

Henry said, "Oh." He was not sure about that. It did not sound fun. Who knows what could be in creek water or lake water? There could be mud or fish or sharp sticks.

Corey said, "It's OK. You can just come with me at first. Stay on the side of the creek and enjoy the water from there. Sugar Creek is a good place to start out. It has clear water. And it's close by. It's not deep. I'll be coming over full days, now that school is out. We'll find lots of stuff to do. We can explore town. We can move some furniture around in your house." Corey looked around the living room. She saw the open places with the missing bookshelves and sofa and piano.

Henry asked, "What about Jet Coffee? Will you be working there?"

Corey answered, "I spoke with your mom about it. She said that three days a week you can come with me. I'll work for Maru-sensei Tuesdays, Thursdays, and Saturdays from three to seven. You can bring your books. We can have dinner there. We can bring some food home for your mom to eat."

More surprises for Dr. Berniece Baker, thought Henry.

At that moment, Bell came into the room.

Corey said, "What's this?" She picked up the cat. "*Pee-yew.* She needs a bath! That's one of our projects today. But first, I need some breakfast and some mocha."

Mocha? thought Henry.

They went into the kitchen. Corey looked in the refrigerator. She took out some things. She made cheese toast. She did not wait to see whether Henry ate his toast. She ate hers while she made the mocha. Henry ate a few bites of his cheese toast without thinking. He was more interested in what Corey was doing than what he ate.

Corey took two jars out of her bag. One was marked "instant espresso." The other was marked "drinking chocolate." She poured some milk into a pan and put it on low heat. Then she watched the pan while the milk heated. She pulled a small shiny whisk from her bag. While the milk heated, she whisked the milk quickly. The whisk made a *clacking* sound against the side of the pan.

She said, "We don't have an espresso machine here. I can't steam the milk like I can at Jet Coffee. But I can still make the milk bubbly if I whisk it." She slowly added the instant espresso and drinking chocolate to the pan. Then she slowly poured everything into two cups. She gave Henry a half cup. Henry drank a little. It was just like being at Jet Coffee for the first time. Once more, it was like having a very strong, nameless memory.

In the distance, Henry heard thunder. He heard wind in the trees outside. The gray clouds had come in over Circletown.

Corey said, "Oh, good. Open the windows. There'll be good smells from the rain."

Henry did. There were.

Chapter Thirteen

If Henry sat in the far corner of Jet Coffee, he could see everything that happened in the café. That is how he saw what happened with Corey's dad.

It was late afternoon and quiet. In an hour, it would be busy with people wanting coffee to wake up a little before an evening baseball game or a movie night. It was June. Now, the sun set late. The sky stayed light for a long time. People stayed out and enjoyed the evenings.

Corey and Maru-sensei were making summer pickles. They cleaned off a few of the tables in the middle of the café. They used the tables to chop vegetables. Henry watched as they cleaned, peeled, and chopped carrots, cucumbers, and some other vegetables he did not know.

Henry picked up a large, white, long vegetable. He asked, "What's this?"

Maru-sensei answered, "A daikon, a kind of radish. You peel it this way." He used a knife to peel away a thin layer. Then he peeled away another very thin layer, like paper. It was white and juicy. "Here. Try this." Henry did. It was a little sweet. Then it was bitter. Then sweet again.

Maru-sensei said, "Daikons are from Japan. But I have a friend in Detroit who can grow them."

Then he took Henry to the kitchen. He had a large pot on the stove. Maru-sensei told Henry, "This is for the pickles. It has rice vinegar, a little sugar, and sea salt. Keep it on low heat. Do not let it boil."

Henry said, "OK. It should not boil."

Maru-sensei said, "Right. Most important thing."

That is how Henry found his special spot in the back corner of the café. Sometimes Henry read his book. Sometimes he got up to check the large pot in the kitchen. He made sure the pot did not boil. That could have gone on forever in the long June afternoon. Except for Corey's father.

The front door of Jet Coffee crashed open. Corey, Maru-sensei, and Henry looked up in surprise. Customers looked up from their tables. A lady spilled her coffee. In the doorway stood a tall man with a dirty red cap. He did not shut the café door. Henry saw a large truck parked on the other side of the street. It was so large that it was stopping traffic behind it. Mound Street was busy, but it was old and narrow. Cars were stuck behind the truck. A few drivers were honking their horns.

Henry put down his book. He moved to where Corey and Maru-sensei were working. He wanted to see this tall man.

The man was looking at Corey. He said in a rough voice, "Girl, you're done here. Come on. We're leaving."

Corey said, "No. I'm not leaving."

The man said, "I'm your father. You're done here. Time for you to be with your family. Not wasting your time in this place. You mind me." He grabbed her arm.

Henry could see Corey's dad was strong. He thought those big fingers were hurting Corey.

Corey did not move an inch. She said "No. I'm not leaving. I know what you have in mind. I'm not leaving town with you. I belong here. In Circletown. This is my place."

Henry thought, *Leaving town? Leaving Circletown?*

Corey's father started pulling her to the open door of the café. Corey pulled back. She said again, "No. This is my place."

Maru-sensei said, "Let go. You are hurting her."

Corey's dad let go of her arm. He made a big fist. He was going to hit Maru-sensei! Henry had seen enough fistfights at school to know. But that is not what happened at Jet Coffee. Suddenly, Corey's father was on the floor of the café. Blood was coming out of his nose. Henry could not believe it. Corey was so fast! She had put her foot behind her dad's leg. At the same time, she had hit him on the nose. He went down, hard.

Jet Coffee was dead quiet. No one said a word.

The big dirty man got up after a minute. He held his hand to his bloody nose and left the café.

Chapter Fourteen

Maru-sensei was the first to move. He went to the café customers and served them fresh coffee. He talked to them in a low voice.

Then Maru-sensei came to Corey. He said, "You did not act until you had to. But when you did, you were smooth, fast. You did not wish to hit your father. I know. Mostly, you used your foot to get him off balance. That is the best way. Now just breathe. Nothing more. I will take care of Henry. He is OK. Everything is OK."

Henry thought, *Did Maru-sensei teach Corey to move that way?* Then he heard Maru-sensei say to him, "Henry. Everything is OK. Turn off the vinegar pot. Go slow. Then we will clean up this blood on the floor. We will take care of Corey. And maybe finish the pickles today, too." Henry looked at Maru-sensei. Maru-sensei looked like usual. After seeing Corey and her dad, Henry should not feel safe at all. Yet after listening to Maru-sensei, Henry felt better.

Henry went to the back to the café. He moved slow, like Maru-sensei said. He turned off the big pot with the rice vinegar and salt and sugar and water. Then he found some cloths for cleaning. He went back to where Corey was standing. He then did something he had never done before. He touched a girl's arm. Corey was shaking a little. Before he knew it, Corey was hugging him a little.

After a minute, he asked, "Are you OK?"

She answered, "No."

Her answer surprised him. People were supposed to say "Yes, I am OK." Corey had answered "No." Yet she stood tall. She was talking to him. She was still Corey.

After a minute Corey said, "Let's make these pickles. I want to take some to your mom after work."

Henry said, "OK."

Corey began to peel and chop vegetables again. She and Maru-sensei carried them to the kitchen at the back of the café. Henry watched as they filled glass jars with the vegetables. They then poured the warm rice vinegar, water, sugar, and salt from the pot over the vegetables. They closed the jars. The put the jars into a cool spot.

It was time for Henry and Corey to go home. The sun had set. A few stars had come out. They turned up one street Henry did not know, and it got very quiet. It was like a door had softly closed. Mound Street should be just behind them. He should hear lots of traffic sounds, but he did not. All Henry could see was dim houses and dark trees. Henry could hardly believe that just an hour before, Corey had been pulling away from her dad in the middle of Jet Coffee. That just an hour before, there had been hard words and blood.

When they got to Henry's house, Henry's mom and a police officer were waiting. Dr. Berniece Baker gave Corey a hug and then Henry a hug. She led Henry into the kitchen and gave him some milk to drink. She said "Henry, the police officer and I are going to talk to Corey for a few minutes, OK?"

Henry asked, "Is Corey in trouble?"

His mom answered, "No." Then she left.

Bell the cat came out of the shadows of the kitchen. She sat at Henry's feet. Henry touched her soft head. Bell shut her eyes and purred. Henry shut his eyes and listened.

Chapter Fifteen

Corey stayed with Henry and his mom. As weeks passed, Henry was no longer surprised to find Corey and Dr. Berniece Baker together in the kitchen at breakfast. Bell the cat would watch from the top of the refrigerator. June became July. Most mornings, Corey had wet hair when Henry sat half asleep at the breakfast table. She had already been wild swimming in a lake or river.

"I have to stay in shape for high school swimming," she told Henry. "You should come with me."

Henry thought about this. Then he said, "OK, but not so early in the morning. Maybe later in the day. Mom, is that OK?"

Dr. Berniece Baker was getting ready to go to college. She did not hear Henry at first. She had her bag with books and pens and papers and a rice ball lunch. She did not think she would like the rice balls, but she would try them anyway. Corey had made the lunch. If *Henry* liked rice balls, maybe she would, too. Dr. Berniece Baker asked, "Did you say something?"

Henry said, "Mom, is it OK if I go swimming with Corey?"

Dr. Berniece Baker said, "Today?"

Corey called out from the stove, "Tomorrow. I'll take him to Sugar Creek. It's safe. There's a good straight path to it right behind your house. I think."

Henry's mom said, "All right, then. I'm going. I'll be home late."

Henry and Corey made breakfast. They made cheese toast and coffee *gyunyu*. As Henry made the toast, he took a deep breath. He asked Corey, "Where is your mother? Where is your dad now? Are you going to stay here? I want you to stay in Circletown. Can you stay in this house with us?"

For a few minutes, Henry heard only the sound of Corey whisking the milk in the pan. Then Corey said, "I've never heard you ask so many questions. You sound like Jake!"

Henry laughed.

Corey said, "I have a mother. But I don't know where she is. I was very little when she went missing. I was with her on the road in front of our house. She had me and a bag with our things. We were walking to town. I think we were going to leave Circletown. She was so unhappy. But then she saw something down a path to the river. She told me to wait. She didn't come back."

Henry waited.

Corey started talking again. "The police found me an hour later at the high bridge. I don't remember how I got there."

"Oh," Henry said.

"No one ever talked about it," Corey said. "Of course, I've looked and looked all over Circletown. I walk all the streets and roads and trails and paths. They're crazy. I never know where they will take me. But I never seem to get completely lost. Still, I've never found her."

Henry listened. He forgot the cheese toast.

Corey said, "You asked about my dad. Well, he's gone. The police told me the truck he drove to Jet Coffee last month was stolen. It was not my dad's. So, he's left Indiana to sell it. That's what he usually does. He steals trucks, then he sells them. He won't be back. So don't worry about him."

Corey was now looking at Henry. Henry stepped back a little. He had to look up, Corey was so tall.

Corey said to Henry, "You've never told me about your dad. What's going on with him?"

Henry felt something hot and sad inside him. He said, "My dad's in New York. I think he won't be back. Like your dad."

Chapter Sixteen

The next day was very warm. By the afternoon, it was so hot that Maru-sensei closed Jet Coffee.

"No one wants coffee in hot weather," Maru-sensei said.

Corey thought this was a good time for Henry to try wild swimming. A nice cool swim? Henry said "yes." But he wanted Jake to come, too. Henry was still a little scared to wild swim. Henry asked Corey if Jake could come. She thought it would be OK. A friend might help Henry feel better about things that scared him.

Corey asked Maru-sensei, "Can I use your phone to call my friend?"

"Sure," Maru-sensei said. He and Corey were packing food in a bag. In the bag were rice balls and summer pickles. There were some pickles left from the day Corey's father came to take Corey away. Jet Coffee's customers loved the pickles. Corey and Maru-sensei were going to make more in a few days.

Henry telephoned Jake. Jake was at home. He *wanted* to go swimming in Sugar Creek.

Jake said, "You know, some people like swimming in creeks."

"Right. We'll come and get you in a little while," Henry said.

"Yeah, in a little while," Jake said. "Could be ten minutes, could be *two days*. You know the streets and paths lately."

It was true. Circletown's streets were worse than ever. Last week, a husband and wife got lost overnight on a picnic. They left on a Thursday on one side of town and then showed up the next morning on the courthouse square. They said they sat down at a park by a forest. Then they walked along a pretty river and found a street they did not know. They saw some old houses, and turned down a street that became a forest path. They got lost. It became dark and they fell asleep. When they woke up, they were in the courthouse square.

Everyone in Circletown heard the story. They shook their heads and laughed a little. Still, Corey and Henry did not want to get lost today. When they left Jet Coffee, they used Mound

Street. Then they turned right on Hill Street. Jake's house was on Hill Street. Corey was almost sure Hill Street would take them to Jake's house.

It was so hot. The orange sun had a strange look. There were no clouds. Henry could feel a storm coming.

"There's a storm coming," Corey said. It was like she could read Henry's thoughts. "Don't worry. The storm is hours away. We have time to swim and get home."

As they walked, they did not see the blue pickup truck on the street behind them. It was moving slowly. Two men sat inside it.

Chapter Seventeen

Jake was waiting for them at his house. The three of them walked to Sugar Creek.

"I know a good way to get there," Jake said. He led Corey and Henry to the end of his street. There was a huge rock there. It was taller than Corey and wider than a car. Jake led them around the rock. Behind the rock was a path into a forest. They went down the path and then down a steep hill. Then they were deep in the forest. Henry could hear the sound of water moving somewhere below. Below him was Sugar Creek. It was beautiful, like moving moonlight and night at the same time. The creek was wide and curved.

Corey, Henry, and Jake got down to the bank of Sugar Creek and stood on a small bit of sand. It was cool down there. Trees stretched out overhead.

"Wow," Corey said. "I've been in Circletown my whole life. I've never seen this part of Sugar Creek before. Is it deep enough to swim?"

"Uh-huh," Jake said. "It isn't deep right here. But if you follow the creek that way, it gets deep." He pointed to the right. Then he pointed to the left. "That way, too. It gets deep."

Henry could see the bottom of the creek. It was rocks and sand. He took his shoes off and walked right into the water. The water was cool. Jake and Corey looked at each other in surprise. Henry was in the water! Henry grinned at them.

"What are you waiting for?" he said.

Jake and Henry splashed in the water. They shouted and laughed. Jake went into the deeper, darker parts of creek. Henry did not follow. Henry did not like the idea of the mud and of animals and tree branches in the dark water.

Corey went swimming down the creek. When she returned, she said, "I'm going to swim up the creek, too. That should take us near your house, Henry. There should be a path up to your backyard. Don't go anywhere, OK? We'll eat when I get back." She started swimming away.

Jake said, "Eat? There's something to eat?"

Corey called back, "I heard you, Jake. Just wait to eat until I get back."

Jake said, "Oh, OK."

Corey laughed as she swam away. Soon she was out of sight around a curve up the creek. Jake and Henry splashed around. It was getting a little dark. Henry could no longer see the sun through the trees. He shivered. It was no longer so hot.

He was about to say something to Jake when Jake spoke. "Who's that?" Jake said. He pointed.

Henry looked up to see two men coming down the path to the creek. It was Corey's father! And that tall, light haired man with him? It was Mark Turnbridge, Corey's brother!

"Well, what we got here?" Mark Turnbridge said. He laughed his cold laugh. Now both men were at the edge of the creek looking hard at the two boys. The boys were in a little luck. They were at the far side of the creek.

For once, Jake's voice was quiet. He said to Henry, "Let's swim. We have to tell Corey."

Henry and Jake started swimming hard into the deep, dark, wild parts of Sugar Creek. They headed toward Henry's house and toward Corey, through the water.

Chapter Eighteen

Henry and Jake swam hard. Henry did not have time to think about the dark water under him and around him. He did not have time to think about the mud or the animals in the water. Instead, he thought about the two Turnbridge men behind him on the creek bank. Mark Turnbridge and Corey's father were dangerous! Henry and Jake needed to get away from them. They needed to swim to Corey. Maybe Corey, Henry, and Jake could get to Henry's house. Would Corey's father try to take her away from Circletown again?

They could hear Mark Turnbridge laughing. "This food sure tastes good!

When I'm done, I'm comin' to hurt you bad! And to get my little sister!" He was going through their things! Henry could hear Corey's father say something, but he could not hear the words. Both Henry and Jake could swim. But they were breathing hard. They could not swim faster than the Turnbridges could run up the banks of Sugar Creek. And they could not see where the men were.

Jake gasped. "Where are those guys? I don't see them. Are they after us?"

"I don't know!" Henry gasped. "Keep swimming. We'll see Corey soon. She'll know what to do."

It seemed like they were swimming forever. It got very dark. Henry heard thunder. Yet it was very still, with no wind. As they swam around the corner, Sugar Creek became wide and smooth.

Henry said, "Look, there's Corey!" Corey was standing on the creek bank not far away. She waved at the two boys. They swam over to her. The bank of Sugar Creek was steep and muddy there. She helped Jake out first. Jake started telling her about her brother and her dad.

Corey did not seem surprised. She said, "Okay, we need to get to Henry's house. It's up there." She pointed up the high hill behind her. Then she saw Henry. He was still in the water.

Henry did not want to get out of Sugar Creek. "There's mud," he said. "I don't want to touch it."

"I know," Corey said. "But there's a mystery. A really big mystery. For me to tell you about it, you have to get out of the water."

A mystery? Henry thought. That, with the idea of two dangerous Turnbridge men, who could be anywhere, got him out of the water. His feet and legs were covered in mud. He felt sick.

"We have to get out of here," Henry said. "I don't know where your father is." There was more thunder. Under the trees, it was very dark, like night.

Corey started walking up a path along the creek. "I think this goes to your house, Henry. I was swimming back to you. Then I saw your cat Bell sitting right here on the creek bank. It's like she was waiting for me. That's the mystery!"

"What?" Henry asked. "Bell's inside the house. She never goes out."

Jake said, "Quiet! I hear them! I hear those men!"

Henry heard them too. They were not far away.

Corey's father shouted, "No more tricks, Corey! Show yourself!"

Corey turned white. She said, "Let's get going."

They came to a fork in the path. One fork went uphill to the left. Another fork went to the right. It looked dark. The path was narrow. Corey, Henry, and Jake jumped at a flash of lightning. It was followed by deep, loud thunder.

"Let's take the left fork," Jake said. "It goes uphill. It's got to go to Henry's house."

But Henry saw something he could not believe! There was his cat

Bell sitting a little way down the *right* fork path. Henry could see black and white fur.

"No," he said. "To the *right*! There's Bell. She's waiting for us."

The three friends turned to the right, walking as fast as they could.

Chapter Nineteen

The three friends walked fast down the dark path. They heard the voices of the Turnbridge men. They were close!

"Keep going!" Corey said.

Henry saw Bell on the path ahead. She went to a large tree that had fallen down many years ago. She waited beside it. But when Corey, Henry, and Jake got there, Henry could not see Bell anywhere. Where was she?

"Can we wait here for a little?" Henry said. "Maybe your dad and brother took the other path. We can hide behind this fallen tree."

"OK," Corey said.

All three listened closely. There was thunder, and some lightning, but no rain, and no wind. Where was the storm? Then they heard Corey's dad and brother.

"They're at the fork in the path," Jake said, quietly.

They waited. Which path would the Turnbridges take? Would they go left? Or would they go right? Their voices changed a little.

"They went left," Jake said.

"Just wait," Henry said.

The two men were fighting. Henry heard, "… go back to the right," and "… no, keep going left." Then, suddenly, their voices stopped. One minute the voices were there. The next minute, the voices were *gone*. It was as though a television had been turned off.

Corey looked at Jake and Henry in shock. "What was that?" she said.

"Circletown?" Henry said. His voice was shaking.

Corey started to walk *back* to the fork in the path.

Jake stood in front of her.

"No. Don't go back there," Jake said.

It started to rain.

Corey gave up. All three ran down the path to Henry's house. At least, they *hoped* it went to Henry's house. In Circletown, you never knew. Finally, the path turned uphill. They were covered in mud, but they were in Henry's backyard.

All the lights were on in Henry's house. Dr. Berniece Baker took one look at them and got some big towels. She hugged them all, even Jake. Jake talked so fast that she got the story from him. Corey and Henry did not have to say a thing. Outside, the wind blew, and thunder shook the house.

Dr. Berniece Baker called the police and Maru-sensei. Henry ran upstairs to check on Bell. Where was she? She was curled up on Henry's bed. She looked at him and yawned. He petted her and she purred. Henry noticed little bits of mud on the floor. Did Bell track those in? Was she out in the woods? Or did Henry track in the mud?

Chapter Twenty

Maru-sensei came and talked quietly to Corey. Then he made hot mocha for everyone. Dr. Berniece Baker said, "I will never get used to children drinking coffee."

Maru-sensei said, "In Japan, children drink light coffee. It does not hurt them. I am making a new children's menu for Jet Coffee. I want customers to bring their kids. Henry has been my test. Whatever he will eat, that is my new menu. Children are the best explorers."

Two police officers arrived. They talked to Corey and Henry's mother.

One officer said, "Mark Turnbridge was let out of jail this morning. If he's saying he wants to hurt Corey, he's going back to jail. As for the older Turnbridge, we had no idea he was back in Circletown. We'll search for them both. But not in this storm. You say they're somewhere under the hill here? Down at Sugar Creek?"

Within an hour, the rain ended. Soon, the police were searching. Near Jake's house, they found the blue pickup truck. Then the police searched the forest paths along Sugar Creek. They found men's clothing—jeans, shirts, boots. They were at the fork in the path in the forest. But they did not find Mark Turnbridge, and they did not find Corey's father.

The next day, the Indiana State Police came. Corey's father had been stealing cars and trucks all over Indiana.

The state police had maps of Circleville. They wanted to help search. But the Circleville police just smiled. Everyone in town knew that maps did not work in Circleville.

Summer got close to fall, and Henry and Jake got ready for school. They walked around the county courthouse square. They bought clothes for school. Henry thought it was time to buy a new baseball glove. He had a few more baseball games to play before winter. One afternoon, Henry and Jake helped Corey and Dr. Berniece Baker move the furniture in the Baker's living room. There were no empty places now. There were places to read and to keep books. Dr. Berniece Baker had gotten a new bookshelf and a sofa.

Henry talked to Corey and his mother. "Is Corey going to stay? I want her to stay," he said.

"I'm not leaving," Corey said.

"She's staying," Dr. Berniece Baker said.

Many years passed, and the Turnbridge men were never seen again. Circletown was—Circletown *is*—an odd place.

Thanks to Joshua Weissman for his YouTube video on making espresso.

Thanks to Seven Miles Coffee Roasters for their YouTube video on making mocha.